Sweet Briar
Goes to Camp

by Karma Wilson ❀ pictures by LeUyen Pham

DIAL BOOKS FOR YOUNG READERS
New York

To children everywhere who have been the last to be chosen for a team and the first to be called a terrible name—I know how you feel!
—K.W.

To Marla Frazee, who saw past my quills to see the artist in me . . .
—L.P.

DIAL BOOKS FOR YOUNG READERS • A division of Penguin Young Readers Group • Published by The Penguin Group • Penguin Group (USA) Inc., 375 Hudson Street, New York, NY 10014, U.S.A. • Penguin Group (Canada), 10 Alcorn Avenue, Toronto, Ontario, Canada M4V 3B2 (a division of Pearson Penguin Canada Inc.) • Penguin Books Ltd, 80 Strand, London WC2R 0RL, England • Penguin Ireland, 25 St. Stephen's Green, Dublin 2, Ireland (a division of Penguin Books Ltd) • Penguin Books India Pvt Ltd, 11 Community Centre, Panchsheel Park, New Delhi - 110 017, India • Penguin Group (NZ), Cnr Airborne and Rosedale Roads, Albany, Auckland, New Zealand (a division of Pearson New Zealand Ltd) • Penguin Books (South Africa) (Pty) Ltd, 24 Sturdee Avenue, Rosebank, Johannesburg 2196, South Africa • Penguin Books Ltd, Registered Offices: 80 Strand, London WC2R 0RL, England

Text copyright © 2005 by Karma Wilson
Pictures copyright © 2005 by LeUyen Pham
All rights reserved
Designed by Teresa Kietlinski
Text set in Plantin
Manufactured in China on acid-free paper

10 9 8 7 6 5 4 3 2 1

Library of Congress Cataloging-in-Publication Data
Wilson, Karma.
Sweet Briar goes to camp / by Karma Wilson ; pictures by LeUyen Pham.
        p. cm.
Summary: When Sweet Briar Skunk goes to day camp, she is torn between her popular new friends and a lonely porcupine she wants to befriend.
ISBN 0-8037-2971-5
[1. Friendship—Fiction. 2. Day camps—Fiction. 3. Camps—Fiction. 4. Skunks—Fiction. 5. Porcupines—Fiction.] I. Pham, LeUyen, ill. II. Title.
PZ7.W69656Su 2005   [Fic]—dc22   2003024017

The illustrations for this book were prepared with watercolors on Arches cold-pressed paper.

Sweet Briar Skunk was bored. It was only two weeks into summer vacation and all her friends were away.

She had played in her sandbox.

She had drawn in her sketchbook.

She had splashed in her wading pool.

She had done it all a hundred times.

"Papa, I'm bored," said Sweet Briar.

Papa said, "Well, Little Squirt, you won't be for long. Day camp starts soon."

"Camp Clover Leaf!" said Mama. "Just the cure for a long, lonely summer."

Sweet Briar knew that four-leaf clovers were lucky. Maybe Camp Clover Leaf would be a lucky place.

But on the first day of camp, Sweet Briar worried.

"What if I have the only flowered swimsuit? What if I'm the only skunk? What if I don't make any friends?"

"Try not to worry," Mama said. "Camp is fun! I know you'll make plenty of friends."

Finally they arrived.

Sweet Briar saw gophers, rabbits, mice, and lots of skunks. She sighed with relief.

Maybe Camp Clover Leaf *was* a lucky place.

Then Sweet Briar saw one prickly porcupine sitting all alone. She was the only porcupine in sight.

Before Sweet Briar could say hello to her, the camp director called, "Gather round, critters. I'm Miss Shamrock.

"Let's play a name game. When you catch the ball, call out your name and pass the ball to somebody new. Soon we'll all know each other."

Sweet Briar worried. What if she couldn't catch the ball?

But when her turn came, she caught the ball nicely, said, "I'm Sweet Briar Skunk," and tossed the ball quickly to the porcupine. When the porcupine caught the ball . . .

POP!

"I'm Petal Porcupine,"
she said. "Sorry about the ball!"
Everyone laughed . . .

everyone except Sweet Briar. She felt awful for Petal.

But Petal gave a small smile and
tried to laugh along. "Now you know,
never toss a beach ball to a porcupine!"
she said.

After the game, Marigold joked about Petal, "Stay away from the poky-pine. Get it? Poky?! Ha ha ha!"

Sweet Briar didn't think Marigold's joke was funny, but she didn't say so. She hoped Petal hadn't heard.

At music, they sang the camp song:
"We're lucky, plucky critters.
Unstoppable go-getters.
We're never, EVER quitters.
HURRAY for Clover Leaf!"
Sweet Briar had so much fun, she
forgot all about Petal.

Later at home, Mama asked, "How was camp?"

Sweet Briar laughed. "I wasn't bored!"

Papa smiled. "Did you make friends?" he asked.

"Oh yes, lots of friends. We played beach ball, sang camp songs, and roasted hot dogs."

"That's great!" said Mama. "I'm glad you had a good first day."

That's when Sweet Briar remembered Petal. *I wonder if Petal had a good first day,* she thought.

The next day at camp, there was a three-legged race.
Sweet Briar was paired with Glory.
Safflower was paired with Petal.

Miss Shamrock said, "Ready, set, GO!"
Safflower and Petal didn't make it past the starting line.
"Ooo! Oh! Ouch!" yelled Safflower.
"Oops," said Petal. "I'm sorry, Safflower."
Safflower snorted. "We lost thanks to you!"

Sweet Briar and Glory won first place!

As everybody admired Sweet Briar's medal, Safflower said,
"That's the last time I race with such a slowpoke."

Marigold giggled. "Slow *poke!* Good one, Safflower."

Sweet Briar frowned. "It's not Petal's fault she has quills."

But nobody listened. "She's just not like us," said Glory.

At campfire, Sweet Briar wanted to ask Petal to sit next to her, but she worried.

What if everybody thinks I'm weird?

Sweet Briar stayed where she was. But she could hear Petal's voice. It was lovely and loud.

Later as they made s'mores, Glory said, "What's the opposite of a nice, soft marshmallow? Petal! Ha ha ha!"

Everybody laughed except Sweet Briar and Petal.

But Petal quickly puffed up her quills and tried to smile. "Porcupines are more like prickly pears!" she said.

At dinner Papa asked, "How was your second day?"

"Good," said Sweet Briar.

"But not great?" asked Mama.

"Pretty good," said Sweet Briar. But she had a feeling that Petal's second day wasn't pretty good.

The next day Miss Shamrock said, "It's so hot. Let's go swimming!"

Sweet Briar was wearing a pretty flowered swimsuit.

Marigold said, "I wish I had a flowered swimsuit."

"Me too!" said Safflower.

Glory said, "It's gorgeous!"

They splished and splashed. They dipped and dived. They had inner tube races.

But when Marigold's inner tube bumped into Petal . . .

BOOM!

Hisssssssssss!

"You popped it!" cried Marigold.

"I'm sorry, Marigold," Petal said. "Porcupines do better with canoes!"

Sweet Briar laughed at Petal's joke, but Marigold just paddled away.

Later during critter craft hour,
Sweet Briar saw Petal sitting alone.

Sweet Briar remembered sitting by herself on
her first day of school because she was the only skunk.
She remembered feeling lonely.

Nobody should have to feel like that, she thought.

Sweet Briar had an idea.

She made her craft from a pinecone.

"What," said Marigold, "is *that*?"

Sweet Briar smiled. "*That* is Petal."

"But why?" asked Safflower.

Sweet Briar took a deep breath and said, "Because I like her."

Glory frowned. "But she's a porcupine. What's to like?"

"She has a nice smile, a pretty voice, she's funny, and she makes me laugh."

Sweet Briar glued the finishing touches on her craft.

As she walked over to Petal,
everyone watched.

Sweet Briar smiled and said, "Petal, I made this for you."
Petal beamed. "It looks just like me! Thanks."
Petal held out a bouquet of paper flowers.

There were lovely yellow marigolds and safflowers, morning glories, and pink sweet briar roses. "I made these for you and your friends," Petal said. "I hoped we could all be friends."

Sweet Briar grinned. "It's beautiful!"

Marigold, Safflower, and Glory walked over. They looked at the bouquet. They looked at Sweet Briar. Then they looked at Petal.

"Wow!" said Marigold. "That's really pretty!"

Safflower said, "Petal is an artist."

Glory nodded. "Could you teach
us how to make them?"

"Sure," Petal said. "Porcupines love flowers.
Especially porcupines named Petal!"
Everybody laughed.

That afternoon at campfire, five friends sang:
"*We'll be best friends forever,*
through good or stormy weather.
We'll always stick together—
HURRAY for Clover Leaf!"

Sweet Briar looked at Petal, who was smiling.
She knew that Camp Clover Leaf *was* a lucky place.